D0964766

WELCOME TO
PASSPORT TO READING
A beginning reader's ticket to a brand-new world!

Every book in this program is designed to build read-along and read-alone skills, level by level, through engaging and enriching stories. As the reader turns each page, he or she will become more confident with new vocabulary, sight words, and comprehension.

These PASSPORT TO READING levels will help you choose the perfect book for every reader.

READING TOGETHER
Read short words in simple sentence structures together to begin a reader's journey.

READING OUT LOUD
Encourage developing readers to sound out words in more complex stories with simple vocabulary.

READING INDEPENDENTLY
Newly independent readers gain confidence reading more complex sentences with higher word counts.

READY TO READ MORE
Readers prepare for chapter books with fewer illustrations and longer paragraphs.

This book features sight words from the educator-supported Dolch Sight Words List. This encourages the reader to recognize commonly used vocabulary words, increasing reading speed and fluency.

For more information, please visit www.passporttoreadingbooks.com, where each reader can add stamps to a personalized passport while traveling through story after story!

Enjoy the journey!

Little, Brown and Company

Hachette Book Group
237 Park Avenue, New York, NY 10017
Visit our website at www.lb-kids.com

Little, Brown and Company is a division of Hachette Book Group, Inc.
The Little, Brown name and logo are trademarks of Hachette Book Group, Inc.

The publisher is not responsible for websites (or their content) that are not owned by the publisher.

First Edition: October 2011

ISBN 978-0-316-18298-0

10 9 8 7 6 5 4 3 2 1

CW

Printed in the United States of America

Meet the Muppets

Adapted by Ray Santos

Based on the screenplay
by Jason Segel & Nick Stoller
illustrated by Kory Heinzen

L B

LITTLE, BROWN AND COMPANY
Boston   New York

Hi, ho, Muppet fans!

Can you find these items in this book?

CHICKEN

PENGUIN

TOILET

TUXEDO

Meet Walter.

Walter feels like he does not fit in,

but he does not know why.

Walter does know that he loves to watch

Kermit the Frog and the other Muppets on TV.

He dreams about meeting them one day.

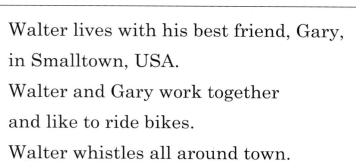

Walter lives with his best friend, Gary,
in Smalltown, USA.
Walter and Gary work together
and like to ride bikes.
Walter whistles all around town.
He likes living there,
but something in his life is missing.

Gary and his friend Mary
know that Walter loves the Muppets.
So the three of them save up their money
and get on a bus to Hollywood.
They are going to make Walter's dream come t
"Muppet Studios, here we come!" Walter chee
as the bus leaves the small town for the big ci

But when they get to Hollywood,

Walter is shocked by what they find.

Muppet Studios is a mess,

and the Muppet Theater is in ruins!

It sure looked a lot better in his dreams.

It clearly has been empty for a long time.

Walter feels sad and wanders off by himself.

Then he hears voices and hides so he can listen.

A man from Texas named Tex Richman

talks to his business partner.

"In two weeks," says Tex,

"we will tear this place down and drill for oil!"

Walter runs to tell his friends the awful news.

He jumps in the car with Gary and Mary.

"We have to go find Kermit!" he yells.

"He can save the Muppet Studios!"

"How are we going to find him?" Mary asks.

"Check a movie-star map?" Walter suggests.

Mary has a better idea. She asks for directions.

At last, they find Kermit's house.

Walter rings the doorbell.

He is nervous. He is going to meet his hero!

"Hi, ho, Kermit the Frog, here,"

Kermit answers.

The famous frog invites them inside.

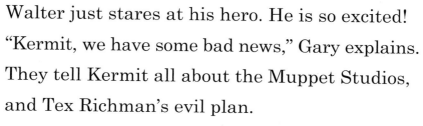

Walter just stares at his hero. He is so excited!

"Kermit, we have some bad news," Gary explains.

They tell Kermit all about the Muppet Studios, and Tex Richman's evil plan.

"We have to put on a show to save the studio," Kermit says.

"But first, we have to find the other Muppets!"

They pile in Kermit's car.

Their first stop is Reno, Nevada.

They find Fozzie Bear performing

with a fake Muppet group called The Moopets.

"Hi, ho, Fozzie," says Kermit. "We need your help."

"But I have this act," says Fozzie.

Then he looks at the sneering Moopets.

Fozzie decides he prefers the Muppets.

With a "Wocka! Wocka!"

Fozzie is ready to join them!

They head out to find Gonzo.

Gonzo used to do daredevil stunts.

Now he runs a plumbing company.

"Have a seat," he says,

offering them toilets to sit on.

Kermit asks him to come back to the Muppets.

Gonzo says, "No. The world needs plumbing."

The Muppets walk outside,
sad to leave Gonzo behind.
But then they hear a voice from above.
"Citizens of Earth! The Great Gonzo is back!"
Gonzo performs a stunt, just like he used to do!
He jumps off the roof in a dive,
holding Camilla the Chicken.

The gang discovers Animal
trying to tame his wild rock-and-roll nature.
"Come on, Animal!" cries Kermit.
"Back to-geth-er?" Animal asks.
"ANIMAL! DRUM?! AYAYAYA!"
Animal shouts.
He waves his arms in the air,
as if he were playing the drums again.

They find Dr. Teeth, Janice, Zoot, and Floyd
from The Electric Mayhem Band rocking out
in the New York subway.
They find Rowlf the Dog relaxing in a hammock.
"Why don't I get this entire page?"
Rowlf asks Kermit.
"We do not have room in the book!" Kermit says.

Walter is so excited.

At last he is meeting all the Muppets!

They find Sam the Eagle hosting a TV news show.

Dr. Bunsen Honeydew and Beaker

are still busy doing experiments together.

Everyone is happy to be back with the Muppets.

Even Sweetums and Swedish Chef hop on board.

The gang makes its last stop in Paris, France.

Miss Piggy works at a fancy French magazine.

Piggy had not seen Kermit in years,

and she missed him.

He would not come with her to France before.

The French like to eat frog legs!

"Miss Piggy," says Walter, "we need you!"

But she will not join them.

"No. I have a life here now," she says sadly.

The Muppets return to the Muppet Studios
without Piggy.

They clean up the theater for the big show.

Walter, Gary, and Mary lend a hand.

"Can you believe it?" Walter asks excitedly.

"We are inside the Muppet Theater!"

The next day the Muppets rehearse.

Even Miss Piggy is back!

She could not let down her friends

(or miss a chance to star in the show).

Everyone is out of practice.

"Walter, can you help us out here?" asks Kermit.

"Share your talent with us."

"Me? I do not have a talent," says Walter.

Walter looks at all the other Muppets.

Fozzie tells jokes to penguins.

Gonzo swings from the rafters.

The Electric Mayhem Band practices with Rowlf.

Kermit tells Walter,

"Just because you have not found your talent yet
does not mean that you do not have a talent.
If you look inside yourself,
you will find something you are good at."

Walter tries really hard to find his talent.

He cannot tell jokes, or do stunts, or play music.

He wishes he could sing and dance like Kermit.

Walter wants to fit in with the Muppets.

Being with them feels like being home to Walter.

But what if he really does not have a talent?

It is finally the night of the big show.
Walter smiles when he sees
how the Muppets are a family.
"What am I going to do?" Walter asks Gary.
"Kermit is wrong. I do not have a talent."

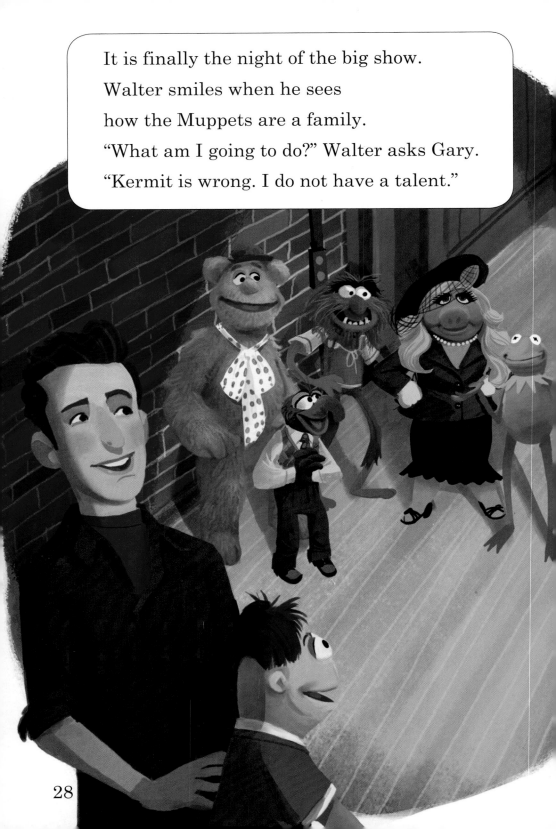

Walter feels terrible.

He does not want to let the Muppets down.

Seeing Walter upset makes Gary feel sad, too.

"Kermit is not wrong," Gary tells him.

Then Gary has an idea.

"Put on your tuxedo, buddy," he says.

"You are up next!"

Walter goes onstage in his tuxedo.

He takes a deep breath

and does what Gary just told him to do.

He whistles a tune.

Walter has always been able to whistle,

but he never thought it was special.

He whistles a beautiful song and everyone cheers.
Walter has a wonderful talent.
And there he is onstage at the Muppet Theater,
performing with the Muppets!

The Muppets found out they still had fans
like Gary and Mary, and they even had a new one!
Tex Richman found himself unable to resist
the humor of the crazy gang.
They did not save the studio,
but in the end it did not matter.
They were happy to have one another.
Walter had a new family in the Muppets,
and Gary was still his best friend.
Not a single thing was missing.